written and illustrated
by
Grandma Magic

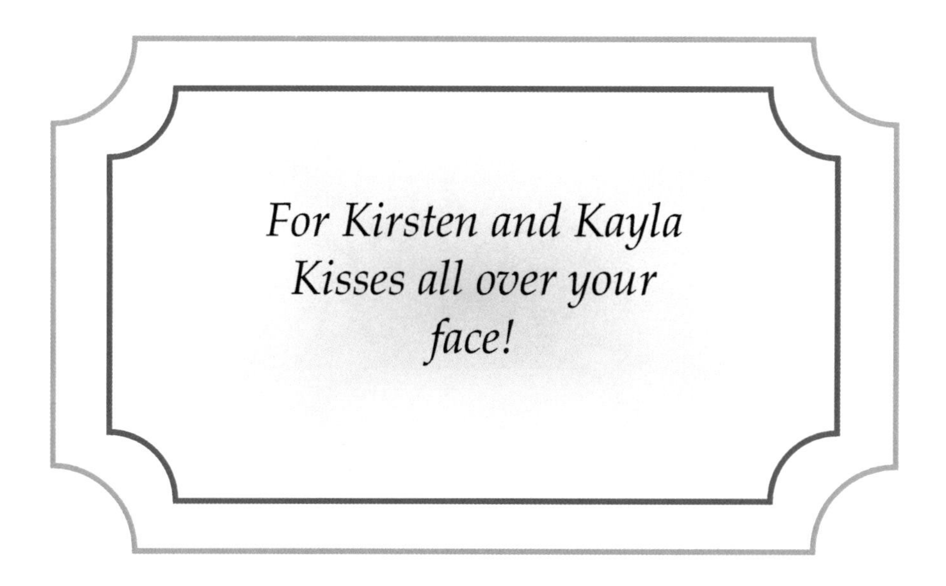
For Kirsten and Kayla
Kisses all over your face!

Twirling Twilly

A little book with a big message

The sun rose out of the dark night sky,
Poking Miss Twilly right in the eye!
The sun climbed higher, to paint the sky blue.
The next thing she knew, morning broke through.

Yawning and blinking, Twilly greeted the day.
Closing her eyes, she said `Grace' over hay.
Her favorite way to welcome the day!
She would think, and thank, and nibble her hay.

It wasn't long before she was done.
Now it was time to have some fun!
She went for a run and a romp through the trees,
Twilly whinnied and rushed up to meet the breeze.
Over the bridge and across the stream,
Tyler waved at Twilly. She was living the dream!

After her fun run, she settled down.
Something caught her eye, near the edge of town.
Scanning the landscape, she saw something funny...
Ears everywhere! It's a field full of bunnies!
Hoping to make friends, away she did go!
She trotted right over to say 'hello'.

"Good morning!" She said, "My name is Twilly.
I live over there! I'm a two-year-old filly."
The bunnies all lined up, from A-Z.
Each bunny was different, it was easy to see!

Each unique bunny had a different skill.
Some jumped around, while others sat still.
Twilly scampered and played with the whole bunny troop.
Bunnies tumbled like acrobats, jumping through hoops!

The smallest blue bunny stayed off to the side.
Not so good at these games, she wanted to hide!
Twilly noticed her sadness and asked her. "Why?"
"Shouldn't you play now, why don't you try?"
The blue little bunny lost her first tear.
"I get teased all the time. Messing up is my fear!"

"My name is Pinky. What sense does that make?
I've had as much teasing as I can take!"
"You can see by my color, my name should be 'Sky'.
Everything about me is wrong... so why even try?!"

"I know what you mean." Twilly smiled her reply.
"But thoughts can be tricky and sometimes they lie!"
"Really?" asked Pinky. "Not ALL thoughts are true?!"
"That's right," answered Twilly. "So here's what to do."

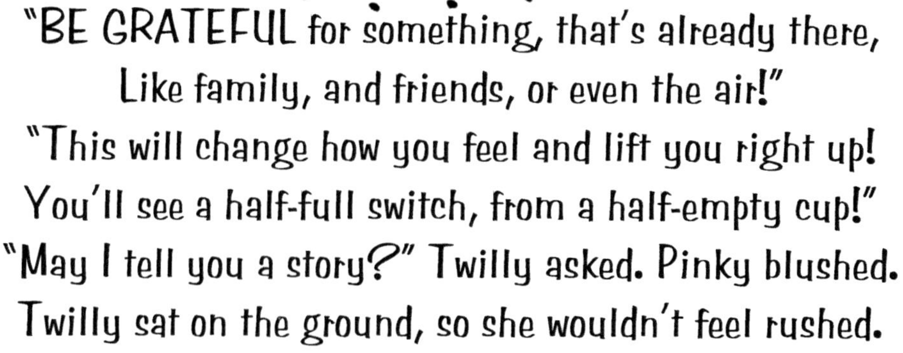

"BE GRATEFUL for something, that's already there,
Like family, and friends, or even the air!"
"This will change how you feel and lift you right up!
You'll see a half-full switch, from a half-empty cup!"
"May I tell you a story?" Twilly asked. Pinky blushed.
Twilly sat on the ground, so she wouldn't feel rushed.

"Tyler, my best friend, planned a carnival day!
Games and prizes galore! We both loved to play!
Balloons popped, bells clanged, and whistles sang out!
If you won a prize, the place exploded in shouts!"

"The face painter painted me all up and down!
Just in time to win tickets, from a friendly clown!
I don't have to tell you, we were feeling our best!
Little did I know, I had started a quest! "

"The air smelled like popcorn and cotton candy!
We shared our treats. Everything tasted dandy!"
"Now the big top show was set to begin.
We went inside, found our seats and then..."

"The spotlight shined down and I dropped my jaw!"
"I couldn't believe all the things that I saw!"
"Elephants danced, and lions roared!
Over our heads, a trapeze family soared!"

"Then out came the horses, dressed for the act!
I was stunned by their beauty, so I made a pact!"
"I vowed I would be like them, right then and there!
I was obsessed with their skill, their glamour, and flair!"

"I was ready to give up my life by the stream
And join the carnival to live out this dream."
"What happened?" asked Pinky, with great big eyes!
Twilly sighed. "This will end, with those thoughts that tell lies."

"I came straight home and packed my bags.
But I needed a costume, I couldn't wear rags!"
"My friends believed, and so did I...
That this was dream I just had to try!"
"I tried on my costume and looked in the mirror...
There was a voice in my head. I still can hear her!"

"She was saying, how silly this could turn out to be.
And that I should give up, so no one would see!
This voice kept telling me how bad I might fail.
These feelings were heavy, like rocks in a pail.
Twilly Sighed."Looking back now, with clearer eyes,"
"I was tricked into quitting, by this one thought that lied!"

"I gave up my dream because fear took its place.
But I learned to be grateful, that's our saving grace!"
"Our gratitude empties the rocks from the pail,
And quiets the voices, that say we might fail."

The more that blue Pinky heard what Twilly said,
The more happy thoughts came into her head!
Pinky started to smile, feeling cheerful and strong.
It turned her bright pink! "I had it all wrong!"

"When my thoughts turn me blue, and drag me down,
There IS a simple way to turn things around!"
"We all have the power to choose what to think!"
"Choose happy and grateful, life will change in a blink!"

"This, sounds important...Folks have to be taught!"
"Everyone should know this." Pinky paused and thought.
"If some thoughts that we think, might not be true...
It can keep us from doing what we really should do!"

"Absolutely!" cheered Twilly, trotting and prancing.
A great idea came to Pinky, when she saw Twilly dancing!
"Do you still have your costume?" Pinky crossed her fingers.
"I have it here in this box, whew... the dust really lingers!"
Twilly blew the dust off with a sneeze and a cough.
Pinky held her breath, as the box top came off.

Inside the box, lay a feathered cap,
With clothes that sparkled and things that snapped!
Pinky laughed, "Let's do it... Let's dress you up!"
"We'll get you started on that half-full cup!"
"You've dreamed of the stage and performing with flair,
I'll be your assistant! We'll make a great pair!"

Twilly got dressed up, twinkling and twirling!
The bunny troop acrobats jumping and whirling!
Something rare and enchanted began to unfold.
Some magic or other, in that moment, we're told;
Not only did Twilly put on her best shine,
Miss Pinky joined in, for the very first time!

The troop practiced daily, getting better and better!
They knew the routine, to the very last letter!
Each bouncing bunny was part of the team.
Working together was really a dream!
The bunny troop balanced on Twilly's strong back!
Climbing higher and higher, they built a tall stack.
To their surprise, Pinky climbed to the top,
Flipping upside down, in one quick hop,
Landing on one little finger, of her little pink paw...
The 'pinky' one! So they made a new law;
That Pinky would be the cherry on top!
They loved to perform and would never stop!

I'll tell you something, and it's a hum-dinger;
Pinky was named ... after her little finger!
If she had stayed blue, she might never know,
Why she was called Pinky, now, the star of the show!
Their friends jumped up, clapping and wowing!
Twilly and bunnies were blushing and bowing!
Everyone cheered to see Twilly this dancy!
She was living her dream to be regal and fancy!

Pinky finally let go of all her fears.
They would do this act for many years.
And Twilly found out, dreams are always waiting.
Keep a grateful heart and no hesitating!
Gratitude is the key that makes life worthwhile!
It's the power to change thoughts and live life with a smile!

Twilly learned a big lesson and told Tyler T...
It's also a lesson for you and me;
That WHAT we think, is a really BIG DEAL!!
It makes all the difference in WHAT we feel!
Remember how LUCKY you are, to be you!
Switch the untrue voice to gratitude!

At the end of the day, when it was time to go...
They flipped a coin; heads/ fast, tails/ slow!
It landed on heads... WHOOSH! Twilly sped by!
And Tyler held tightly...'cause
TURTLES DON'T FLY!!

A Note From Grandma Magic

*The 'half-full/half-empty glass' analogy is about perspective.
Please consider that both are true; the glass is indeed half-full
and half-empty, simultaneously.
The free will of humans, gives everyone the choice,
of either viewpoint .
It is like a lens that colors our view of the world,
otherwise, known as an optimistic or pessimistic outlook.
Perhaps this skill could be learned at an early age?
Children accept these concepts at face value.
A grateful heart sees the glass half-full!
It's very simple, but simple, doesn't necessarily mean it's easy!*

About the Author

Debbie Wolski is a yoga instructor and Studio owner who loves art, family, and the creative process!

The mandatory 2020 shutdown of her California business, Village Yoga Center, prompted her to create the characters of Grandma Magic and the charming woodland creatures with whom she interacts.

As a great-grandmother of 6, and counting, she looks to create a brighter future for her children's children's children. "My goal is to make the world a better place," she admits, "by sending positive, insightful messages through these quirky characters."

"I hope these simple loving concepts and life lessons have a profound impact on young minds and the adults around them!"

Fun Tongue Twister

Twilly loved to twirl!
Twilly twirled and whirled around the world!
The more Twilly twirled, the more the world whirled.
The wide world whirled as twirling Twilly twirled!

Made in the USA
Middletown, DE
07 September 2024